each day . . .

the wonderful

cynthia rylant

illustrated by

coco dowley

happens

aladdin paperbacks

new york   london   toronto   sydney   singapore

in a little kitchen
someone butters bread,
wonderful bread.

the earth grew wheat,
the wheat made flour,
and the wonderful happened:

bread.

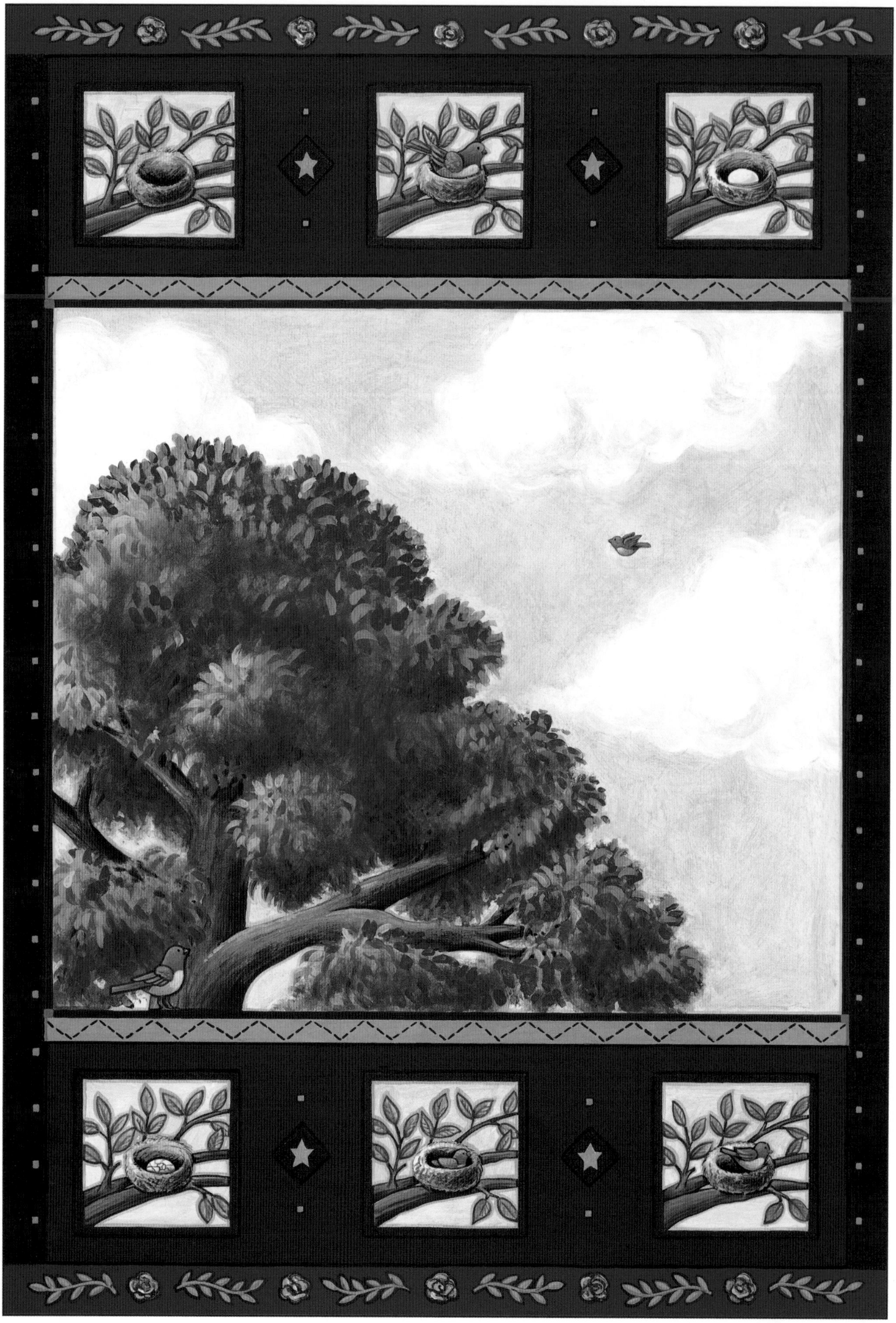

in a wide blue sky
flies a tiny bird,
a wonderful bird.

it was an egg,
then it hatched,
and the wonderful happened:

a bird!

up a white fence
climbs a red red rose,
a wonderful rose.

someone loved flowers
and asked a seed to grow
and the wonderful happened:

a rose.

the wonderful happens every day:

peaches grow,
bees buzz,
and it rains.

water makes tea,
apples make pie,
and it snows.

dogs sit, clouds glide,
new spiders
spin their very first webs.

cats look out windows,
stars glow,
and squirrels sleep
in treetop beds.

there is ivy,
there are worms,
there are clocks that keep time.
there's a moon lighting up a night sky.

and most of all and best of all,
it all never ends,
for the wonderful happens
and happens again:

pie
cats
apples
clocks
tea
dogs
ivy
birds
wheat
and
peaches
and
you.

yes: **you.**

did you know
there was a time
when you weren't anywhere?

but you happened
like bread,
like a bird,
like rain,

you happened
like peaches and snow.

the wonderful happened,
the wonderful is **you.**
growing like a red red rose.

For Verité and Skyla

—C. R.

For Luke and Rose with special thanks to Tracy

—C. H. G. D.

First Aladdin Paperbacks edition November 2003

ALADDIN PAPERBACKS
An imprint of Simon & Schuster
Children's Publishing Division
1230 Avenue of the Americas
New York, NY 10020

Also available in a Simon & Schuster Books for Young Readers hardcover edition.
Designed by Anahid Hamparian
The text of this book was set in 36-point Berliner Grotesk.

Manufactured in China
4 6 8 10 9 7 5

The Library of Congress has cataloged the hardcover edition as follows:
Rylant, Cynthia.
The wonderful happens / by Cynthia Rylant ; illustrated by Coco Dowley.
p. cm.
Summary: Describes some of the things that bring happiness and awe into our lives, including a baby bird,
fresh-baked bread, snow, clocks, the moon, and more.
ISBN 0-689-83177-3 (hc.)
[1 Wonder Fiction.] I. Dowley, Coco, ill. II. Title.
PZ7.R982Wo 2000
[E]—DC21
99-31241

ISBN 0-689-86355-1 (Aladdin pbk.)